The PRINCESS And the PENGUINS

Written by
Rosa Roberts-Johnson

Illustrations by
Annie Grant

DJD Publications
Jacksonville, Florida

The Princess and the Penguins
DJD Publications
Jacksonville, Florida
cococamwrites@aol.com

All rights reserved. This book is protected under the copyright laws of the United States of America. No part of this book may be reproduced or transmitted in any form or by any means – electronic or mechanical, including photocopying, recording or by any information storage and retrieved system without written permission from the authors, except for the inclusion of brief quotations in a review.

This is a work of fiction. Names, characters, places, businesses and incidents either are products of the author's imagination or are used fictitiously and are not to be construed as real. Any resemblance to a real person, living or dead, business establishments, actual events, locales, or organizations is entirely coincidental and not intended by the author.

DJD Publications Books are available at special discounts for bulk purchases. Contact: Coco at cococamwrites@aol.com

Copyright © 2016 Coco
ISBN #: 978-0-9861251-0-2
Library of Congress Control Number: 2016947605
Printed in the United States of America

DEDICATION

This book is dedicated to my she-ro, my princess, my mother! Words cannot express how much I love her!

To every little girl in the world who feels that she is not pretty enough, YOU ARE ENOUGH. A princess lives inside of each and every one of you. Remember that EXTRAORDINARY doesn't fit. Be true to who you are always.

- Coco

Today; tomorrow will be your future. Tomorrow; today will be your past. Be productive in your past, to make your future attainable.

- Coco

Acknowledgments

Where do I start? I guess I would have to say that my first inspiration for writing this book would be my love for children and my love for the color Pink and what it represents: Breast Cancer. Breast cancer touched close to home for me with my mother and I am proud to say that she is a SURVIVOR!

Secondly, I would say, my love for all the princesses in my life; my nieces! Latavia "Paris" Gadson, Drucilla "Plus Size Barbie" Gadson, Mya Edwards, Torrance "Torr" Roberts, Salaa "LaaLaa" Johns Tamarae "Olive Oil" Roberts, Imajah Roberts, Zion "Mouth of the South" Roberts, and last but not least my lil shorty, doo-whop herself Ylizabeth "Minnie Mouse" Merkinson! My Goddaughter(s) Datasha "Tasha" Mitchell, Krishayne' "Shane" Mitchell and Nylah "Dimples" Capers! I am a Glam-ma ya'll; to one beautiful little ladybug; Rheagann Peola Lettingham!

Last but not least, my beautiful mother, who now rests in heaven. I love you mommy. Fly high and live free. My love for you is engraved in my heart as long as it beats.

I hope that you and all the princesses in your life enjoy!

Princess Leah and her mom went to town for a day of shopping. Leah let go of her mom's hand for a little while so that she could watch the animals doing tricks on the snow.

Before she knew it, she had wandered too far. Leah walked until she came upon a sign that read Guzza. She began to cry. How would she get back home? She was scared, cold and lonely.

Leah, walked until she was tired, so she looked for a place to rest. She gathered some snow, just enough to make a small pillow. Leah, pulled her hat down over her little face as far as she could, wrapped her scarf around her neck to make sure that she was nice and warm, tugged on her mittens, laid her head on the snow and drifted off to sleep.

Suddenly she felt a nudge at her feet. With sleepy eyes, she looked to see a family of Penguins surrounding her. *Black* and *White* Penguins. Startled, she sprang to her feet! Looking around for a place to run. One of the Penguins spoke, "Don't be afraid."

"Did you just talk?"

"I did," The penguin said.

"But you're a penguin."

"Here in the land of Guzza, animals have the ability to speak. I'm Jay." He introduced himself. "These are my brothers, Dee and Monny."

"Hi, how are ya?" Dee spoke. He was goofy, the funny one.

"Hey." Monny spoke, he was the shy one.

"Hi Jay, Monny, Dee, nice to meet you, I'm Leah." They immediately bonded and became friends.

"You aren't from Guzza are you?" Jay asked.

"Nope." Says Leah. "I was watching the animals do tricks on the ice and before I knew it, I wandered too far."

"You were probably watching me." Dee says with his chest poked out.

"No offense, but you all look the same, so I don't know who I was watching." Monny and Jay laughed so hard, they fell over on the ice.

"Well, when you see a Penguin slipping and sliding, dancing and jiving, you know that it's me, the big Dee."

"Showoff," Monny mumbled.

"Well, welcome to Guzza, we will take good care of you until we can get you back to your family," Jay says.

The Penguins helped Leah build an Igloo house so that she could have a place to sleep.

They showed her how to fish, so that she could eat and they made snow angels, went ski boarding and had a snowball fight!

For the moment Leah was comfortable in her surroundings. She was no longer afraid or alone, she was happy; she was having fun.

The next day Leah was inside her Igloo, and thought to herself, *I wish there was more color around here.* She walked in circles trying to figure out how she could make her Igloo a little cozier, like her room in Tizzalville. As she walked in circles, there was a knock at the door. "Come in." It was Jay.

"Hi Leah."

"Hi Jay," She says, still walking in circles.

"Why are you walking in circles?"

She stopped. "I'm trying to figure how to make it colorful in here. Her eyes lit up when she said the word colorful!

Bursting in the door without knocking, enters Dee as he blurts out, "Well, make it colorful." Monny walked in behind him, nibbling on a small fish that he caught. Jay saw the excitement in Leah's eyes, every time the word colorful was mentioned.

"How can I get color? There is no color around here. Everything is *White*, except for you guys, and you're *Black* and *White*."

"Across the big, *Blue*, Ocean, there is a place that has lots of color!" Said Jay.

"Really?" Leah exclaimed!   Excited about what she was about to see; she began to dance.

Dee joined her. "Go Princess, get down with your bad self." Jay and Monny, just watched and giggled.

"Wait.   How will we get across the Ocean? Have you guys ever been to this land?"

"We don't go on the land, but we go over to lay on the snow and people watch. Maybe you will see your family," Monny said.

Leah didn't think about her family being across the ocean; but she was sure that they were looking for her. Excited about being able to have color in her Igloo, she asked, "When can we leave?"

"Now." Jay was calm when he spoke, but it gave his heart joy to see how excited she was.

Skipping around, she said, "Let's go!"

"We wanna go!" Blurted Dee and Monny.

"Calm down. Hop on." She hopped on his back and they headed across the ocean.

The moment they arrived, Leah's mouth flew open. Leah realized that the town Jay took her to, was Tizzalville. "Will you come with me?"

"No Leah, we must stay here."

She smiled and said, "I'll be right back." Leah walked through the streets of the town, looking in window after window, smiling the whole way.

She came upon the fabric store and went inside. Her heart was filled with joy, there were so many colors! With Leah being gone a whole day, her clothes and hair were different, no one noticed that she was the Princess. As Leah was walking through the store, running her hand across the beautiful, fabric, not paying attention, she bumped into a woman. "Oh I'm very sorry ma'am."

The woman turned around and was very surprised. "Leah!" She said with tears in her eyes. "Where have you been?"

Leah looked up and saw her mother. "Mother!" She screamed and threw herself into her arms "Mother, did you look for me?" She asked through tears. "I was so scared; I didn't know what to do. I was watching the Penguins do tricks on the ice and before I knew it, I wandered too far."

"Oh hunnie, we looked for you, day and night. It doesn't matter now, you're here."

Leah squeezed her mother tightly. She didn't want to let her go. "Mother, I'm so happy to see you. If I knew this was the way home, I would have come back yesterday." After seeing her mother, Leah forgot about the reason she was in the store.

Leah and her mother were leaving the store when it hit her. She had come there with Jay and his brothers. *What would she say to them?* She stopped, looked at her mother with sadness in her eyes. "What's the matter Leah?"

"Mother, I came here with someone. I have to say goodbye to them."

Leah's mother looked puzzled, but she didn't say anything. She grabbed her daughter's hand and walked with her towards the snow bank where Jay, Dee and Monny were sitting. As Leah approached the snow bank, Jay could see the tears in her eyes.

"Hey guys, I have found my family, I am home."

Jay didn't say anything, he just watched as she talked. Monny started shuffling his feet a little, Dee was happy for her, he had a big smile on his face. "I didn't know this was the way home. I'm sorry; I can't go back with you."

Leah said sniffling. Jay turned and started making his way back home. Monny and Dee followed.

Leah yelled. "I won't ever forget you guys; I will miss you!"

Leah returned home with her mother and her family was very happy to see her; but she felt out of place. She didn't know this feeling.

One day when Leah returned to the fabric store with her mother, she glanced over at the snow bank and knew what she was missing.

Leah ran out of the fabric store towards the icy, snow bank. "Leah!" Her mother called out. "Where are you going?"

"Mother, I have to return to my friends."

"You don't know what you're saying. They are just animals!"

She stopped and caught her breath. "Mother, when I was lost, they took care of me. They built me a home; they showed me how to fish, snow board, everything. I did things that a Princess is never allowed to do." Without saying another word, Leah ran into the snow, making her way back to the town of Guzza. "I will return."

When Guzza was in her sight, she called out for Jay. "Jay, I'm here, I've come back. Monny. Dee." No one answered. She called out for them again. "Jay, where are you? Monny, Dee, where are you guys?" Still no answer. Leah became very sad and began to cry, but she kept walking.

Leah wandered around for a while, until she reached her Igloo. She stepped inside and was in awe. There sat Jay; it was colorful!

"Jay." She said softly. "I called out for you."

Jay stood with a smile on his face. "Princess, you've come back. What are you doing here? What about your family?"

"You are my family too Jay. So are Monny and Dee. I've missed you; I've missed the Igloo, snowboarding and snowball fights." Jay and Leah hugged. When they broke their embrace, Leah stood back to see all the wonderful things that Jay had done to the Igloo. He had filled the house with beautiful shades of *Pink*.

"I didn't know what colors you liked, so I picked the colors that I thought fit you. Monny and Dee helped, of course. I see you as my pretty, pink, ice Princess." Leah walked around the Igloo admiring what her friends had done.

"Do you like it?" Jay asked.

"I love it! It's beautiful!"

"I wanted something to remember you by."

Smiling she said, "Thank you. "Jay, I cannot stay, my family would miss me I promise to visit every chance I get."

"Leah, I did not plan for you to return, so it's ok. Your Igloo will always be here; we will always be here. I love you."

Dee and Monny peeked around the corner. They ran over and gave Leah a hug. "We love you too."

Embracing her friends, she says, "I love you all."

ABOUT THE AUTHOR

Rosa Roberts-Johnson (Coco) is a mother to many and a friend to all. Her love for children is what has inspired her to write her first children's book. Coco fell in love with writing at a very young age. Making greeting cards for her mother (for any holiday) and writing poems.

Coco self-published her first novel, Losing Yourself, in 2012, following up with this children's book. She has the desire to write many more children's books, as well as other books, that will teach and inspire.

CPSIA information can be obtained
at www.ICGtesting.com
Printed in the USA
LVHW07s2147200918
590858LV00010B/36/P